SURPRISE PACKAGE

by mort walker

A TOM DOHERTY ASSOCIATES BOOK

This is a work of fiction. All the characters and events portrayed in this book are fictional, and any resemblance to real people or incidents is purely coincidental.

BEETLE BAILEY: SURPRISE PACKAGE

First printing: July 1984
Second printing: October 1985

A TOR Book

Published by Tom Doherty Associates
49 West 24 Street
New York, N.Y. 10010

ISBN: 0-812-56092-2
CAN. ED.: 0-812-56093-0

Printed in the United States

0 9 8 7 6 5 4 3 2

GOOD JOB, MEN
NOW WE CAN HAVE A LITTLE FUN AROUND HERE
24-HOUR CRAP GAMES
I CAN FINISH MY SET OF GREAT BOOKS
SLEEP TILL NOON!
MAYBE I DO NEED A GOOD REST
I COULDN'T THINK OF ANYTHING TO YELL AT THEM ABOUT

BOY! I CAN'T FIND ANYTHING IN THE DARK
THE WAY EVERYONE IS SNORING, THIS LIGHT SHOULDN'T BOTHER THEM
CLICK
HEY! WHO TURNED ON THE LIGHTS?!
I'M LOOKING FOR MY FOOTLOCKER KEY. I CAN'T GO TO BED WITHOUT BRUSHING MY TEETH

WHAT'S ALL THE YELLING? I WAS SOUND ASLEEP
HUH? IS IT TIME FOR REVEILLE ALREADY?!
REVEILLE? DID SOMEONE CALL REVEILLE?
MY CLOCK MUSTA STOPPED! OKAY, MEN! UP AND AT 'EM!!

ADAMS... ADORNEY... AXTELL...
HERE
HERE
HERE
HOLD IT, SARGE! WHO JUST TURNED OUT THE LIGHT IN THE BARRACKS ?
CLICK
I'LL KILL HIM!
WAIT TILL MORNING. HE'D NEVER KNOW IT IF YOU KILLED HIM NOW
MORT WALKER 11-26
Z

THE END

DOESN'T ANYONE KNOW ANY FUNNY STORIES?
US
US
US
US
US
US
US
US
US

THE WALLPAPER HAS FLOWERS ALL OVER IT EXCEPT FOR A BIG EMPTY SPACE WITH ONE LITTLE FLOWER ALL BY ITSELF

I DON'T THINK THAT'S VERY FUNNY
IT'S NOT BAD FOR A WALLPAPER GAG
MORT WALKER
12-10

THE END

I THINK BETTER WITH MY FEET ELEVATED
SARGE

SARGE!!
HE'S ASLEEP, SIR. DO YOU WANT ME TO WAKE HIM UP?
NO
I'LL WAKE HIM!!

WHOOSH
MORT WALKER
© 12-17
© King Features Syndicate, Inc., 1972. World rights reserved.
HE HAS VERY STRONG ANKLES, SIR

THE END

GROWL
Z Z.... HUH?
DARN! NOTHING LEFT BUT CRUMBS!
SNAX
BOY, IF I WAS MARRIED NOW I WOULDN'T HAVE TO GET OUT OF BED ON A COLD FREEZING NIGHT LIKE THIS

I'D JUST SAY TO MY WIFE, "GO DOWNSTAIRS TO THE KITCHEN AND FIX ME A HOT CUP OF COCOA"
U.S.
BUT WHERE AM I? I'M IN AN ARMY BARRACKS WITH SIXTY OTHER STUPID JERKS LIKE MYSELF
I'M THE ONE WHO HAS TO GET OUT OF BED

OH, WELL IT COULD BE WORSE
© King Features Syndicate, Inc., 1972. World rights reserved.
12-24
MORT WALKER
Z-.. HUH?
BEETLE! GO OVER TO THE MESS HALL AND TELL COOKIE TO FIX ME A HOT CUP OF COCOA

THE END

BEETLE! YOU'RE SUPPOSED TO BE WASHING WINDOWS!
GIVE ME THAT GLOVE AND BAT!
SARGE! YOU'RE SUPPOSED TO BE WORKING ON A REPORT! PUT DOWN THAT GLOVE AND BAT!
BUT...
PLAYING BALL DURING DUTY HOURS! I WON'T HAVE IT!!

I'LL BE DARNED, SIR! DID YOU SEE THAT?
WOW!
HOW DID THAT HAPPEN ?
WHEN YOU HIT THE DESK, YOUR FIST CAME DOWN ON THE RULER, WHICH WAS RESTING ON AN ERASER--- THE OTHER END OF THE RULER WAS UNDER THE COFFEE CUP
I SEE... IT CATAPULTED THE CUP ONTO THE SHELF, KNOCKING OFF THE BOOKEND, WHICH HIT YOUR BAT, SENDING IT SPIRALING OUT THE WINDOW

I'LL BET YOU COULD NEVER DO THAT AGAIN IN A MILLION YEARS! IT MUST BE SOME KIND OF A WORLD'S RECORD!
GOSH!
© King Features Syndicate, Inc., 1972. World rights reserved
I HOPE THE GENERAL HEARS ABOUT THIS!
MORT WALKER 12-31

THE END

RUSH THIS THROUGH
YES, SIR
RUSH THIS THROUGH
YES, SIR
RUSH THIS THROUGH
"STUDY OF HOW SOLDIERS RELAX"?

IT SEEMS LIKE EVERYONE IN THIS WHOLE COUNTRY IS ALWAYS RUSHING!
I WONDER WHY?
HQ
EVERY WEEK I SAY, "THIS IS THE WEEK I'M GOING TO GET MY WORK CAUGHT UP!"
IN
OUT
THEN SGT. WEBBING CALLS WITH AN EXTRA TICKET TO THE BALL GAME OR SOMEONE ASKS ME TO GO BOWLING OR TO THE MOVIES... IT'S ALWAYS SOMETHING!

WELL, I DON'T CARE WHO CALLS...
THIS IS THE WEEK I'M GOING TO GET MY WORK CAUGHT UP!!
CLIK!
WELL...?
MORT WALKER
THE END
1-5

WE HAVE A PROBLEM, GENERAL
WHAT IS IT, MY DEAR?
THREE TIMES AS MANY GIRLS SHOWED UP FOR OUR LECTURE AS WE COUNTED ON. WE NEED A LARGER PLACE.
WHAT KIND OF LECTURE IS IT?
LOVE AND MARRIAGE
HOW ABOUT THE FIELD HOUSE ?
US

I THINK THE GYM IS THE PERFECT PLACE FOR OUR DISCUSSION GROUP ON MARRIAGE
FINE. LET ME HOOK UP THE MIKE FOR YOU
OOPS! I BLEW A FUSE!
ZAP!
US
JUST SIT TIGHT, GIRLS. I THINK THE FUSE BOX IS BACK HERE
THAT WAS A HOT GAME OF HAND-BALL, SNORKEL
YEAH. AND DO I NEED A SHOWER

HEY! SOMETHING'S WRONG WITH THE LIGHTS
NEVER MIND. WE CAN FIND OUR LOCKERS IN THE DARK
CLICK CLICK
© King Features Syndicate, Inc., 1969. World rights reserved
CLICK
GASP
I FIXED THE FUSE. AREN'T YOU GOING TO HAVE THE MEETING?
WE LEARNED ENOUGH FOR ONE NIGHT
1-12
MORT WALKER
THE END

I WONDER IF SARGE FOUND THAT SIGN WE PUT ON THE BULLETIN BOARD
SGT. SNORKEL was A NURSERY SCHOOL DROPOUT
FALL OUT!
HE FOUND IT!

WHOEVER WROTE THIS ON THE BULLETIN BOARD BETTER CONFESS OR I'LL PUT THE WHOLE STUPID BUNCH OF YOU ON K.P.!!

SGT. SNORKEL WAS A NURSERY SCHOOL DROPOUT

BO-IIING!

THAT-WAS-NOT-VERY-BRIGHT! ALL I HAVE TO DO NOW IS FIND THE GUY WITHOUT A HELMET!

ALL RIGHT! WHO BROUGHT ALONG TWO HELMETS?!!
MORT WALKER
THE END
1-19

SHHH
WHY ARE WE TIPTOEING? SARGE ISN'T ANYWHERE AROUND
I KNOW, BUT HE CAN SMELL CAKE A MILE AWAY. SHHH
I WANT TO GET A KNIFE AND HAVE ONE PIECE BEFORE HE GETS HIS FACE IN IT

YOU SHOULDN'T POINT THAT GUN TOWARD THE BIVOUAC AREA
IT WON'T HURT. I'M ONLY USING BLANKS
BUT BEETLE HID HIS CAKE FROM SARGE IN THE BARREL
BOOM

DARN! MY SHOE IS UNTIED

WHEW! I THINK I'LL SIT DOWN A MINUTE

HEY! THERE'S A PENNY

AH, WHAT A BEAUTIFUL DAY...
© King Features Syndicate, Inc., 1969. World rights reserved
1-26

I KNEW IT! THE MINUTE MY BACK IS TURNED HE'S GOT HIS FACE INTO MY CAKE
THE END

MMM

BOY! I'D SURE LIKE A DATE WITH HER!
I KNOW HER. LET ME FIX YOU UP

NOT BAD. I MIGHT EVEN BUY HER A SODA BEFORE I TAKE HER TO LOOKOUT POINT

I TRIED TO FIX YOU UP BUT SHE'S VERY FUSSY WHO SHE DATES
YEAH? WELL, I DON'T GIVE UP THAT EASY
WELL, I GUESS NO ONE ELSE IS GOING TO SHOW UP
APPLY FOR PARA-TROOPS HERE
WELL, BABY, HERE I AM! LOOK ME OVER
FIRST SIT DOWN AND FILL OUT THIS QUESTIONNAIRE
YOUR MEDICAL RECORD SEEMS SATISFACTORY. JUST A FEW TESTS I'D LIKE TO MAKE
DO YOU JUMP MUCH?
ONLY IF YOU HAVE COLD HANDS

DO YOU APPROVE OF MANY GUYS?
NOT MANY. WHEN THEY FALL I WANT TO MAKE SURE THEY ARE PERFECT SPECIMENS
I DON'T KNOW IF IT'S WORTH IT
DON'T GIVE UP NOW. YOU'VE ALMOST GOT IT MADE
© King Features Syndicate, Inc., 1969. World rights reserved
MORT WALKER
I WONDER WHAT THE POOR GUY WHO WANTS TO MARRY HER WILL HAVE TO DO?
THE END
2-2

GARAGE

THUNK
GARAGE

DON'T TELL ME, LET ME GUESS...SARGE SENT YOU OVER TO FIX HIS BRAKES
YEAH. HOW DID YOU KNOW?

HEY! I THOUGHT SARGE WANTED YOU TO FIX HIS BRAKES!
I KNOW. BUT I WANT TO SOUP UP THE MOTOR FIRST
GARA
I'LL WORK ON THE BRAKES AFTER LUNCH
MOTOR POOL
GOOD! IT LOOKS LIKE HE'S DONE WITH MY JEEP! I GOTTA GET TO THAT MEETING!
WHAT WAS THAT?
PROBABLY JUST A BIG GUST OF WIND
ZOOM

THE BRAKES DON'T WORK! I'LL JUST HAVE TO DRIVE IN CIRCLES TILL I RUN OUT OF GAS!

THAT'S THE SECOND TIME THAT SPEED DEMON NEARLY HIT US
WE SHOULD REPORT HIM TO SARGE

MAYBE IF I HIT THAT BIG PILE OF LAUNDRY BAGS--
© King Features Syndicate, Inc., 1969. World rights reserved.

HEY, SARGE! WAIT TILL YOU SEE WHAT I'VE DONE TO YOUR JEEP---
--WHY ARE YOU WEARING SHORTS ON YOUR HEAD?
THE END
MORT WALKER
2-9

(SIGH)
IT'S THAT DAY AGAIN
FEBRUARY 1969
(SIGH)
IT'S THAT DAY AGAIN
WAKE UP! IT'S THAT DAY AGAIN
SIGH

NOW, TRY TO BE NICE TO THE SERGEANT.. BEETLE IS IN ENOUGH TROUBLE ALREADY
TRY TO BE NICE TO MY FOLKS, SARGE. NO MATTER WHAT YOU THINK OF ME, THEY LOVE ME
WELL, WELL. ALWAYS A PLEASURE TO SEE THE MAN WHO TAKES SUCH GOOD CARE OF OUR SON
IT'S..ER..NICE TO MEET THE PARENTS WHO PRODUCED SUCH A (COFF) BOY.
OH, WE CAN'T TAKE ALL THE..UH..CREDIT. I'M SURE YOU HAVE ..MMM..HAD AN INFLUENCE ON HIM
VERY LITTLE, HA! HA! BUT YOU CAN GO HOME KNOWING THAT HE'S.. ER...HIGH ON MY LIST

WHEW! I'LL BE BACK IN A MINUTE
I KNOW WHAT I NEED
MORT WALKER

BARTENDER! GIVE ME A DOUBLE..

PARENTS' DAY IS TOUGH ON EVERYBODY
2-16

THE END

YOU'RE NOT WATCHING THIS, ARE YOU, ZERO?
CLICK

I GUESS NOT

CLICK
CLICK

HOW CAN YOU WALK IN HERE WHILE WE'RE WATCHING A PROGRAM AND JUST SWITCH CHANNELS?

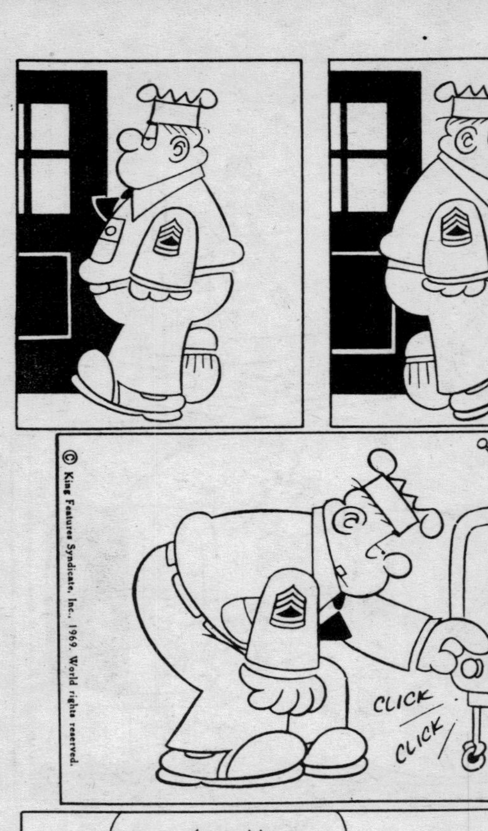

CLICK
CLICK
LIKE THAT
NORT WALKER
THE END
2-23

I DON'T KNOW WHY I'M ALWAYS SO ANXIOUS TO SEE IF THERE'S A LETTER FROM THE PENTAGON
THEY NEVER WRITE ME

I CAN'T WAIT!!
GENERAL HALFTRACK

I CAN'T OPEN IT
GENERAL HALFTRACK

HOT DARN!
A LETTER
FROM THE
PENTAGON!!
GENERAL
HALFTRACK

Dear General:
GENERAL
HALFTRACK

THEY CALLED
ME "DEAR."

Dear General:
In the future, all correspondence from you should be addressed to the office in charge of defunct camps.
US
GENERAL HALFTRACK
WELL, ANYWAY, THEY CALLED ME "DEAR"
GENERAL HALFTRACK
THE END
MORT WALKER
3-2

DO YOU THINK WE'LL EVER GET ENEMY INVADERS AROUND HERE ?
GUARD
ARE YOU KIDDING?

WHO WOULD EVER WANT TO CAPTURE THIS MOSQUITO-INFESTED MUD BOG?
WELL, WE'D BETTER BE ALERT, ANYWAY, IN CASE ONE OF THE OFFICERS COMES BY

I THINK I'LL SEE IF OUR GUARDS ARE ON THE ALERT
US

HALT AND GIVE THE PASSWORD
PEA SOUP

YOU GOTTA BE CAREFUL, BEETLE. SOMETIMES THE ENEMY CAN SPEAK A LITTLE ENGLISH...AND THERE ARE LOTS OF WAYS HE CAN OVERHEAR THE PASSWORD

OKAY. I'LL GIVE HIM A TEST TO SEE IF HE'S REALLY AN AMERICAN
WHERE'S THE STATUE OF LIBERTY?
NEW YORK
WHAT'S A BLT?
A BACON, LETTUCE AND TOMATO SANDWICH
WHO WON THE SERIES?
DETROIT

GUAR
WHAT'S THE TITLE OF THE LATEST SIMON AND GARFUNKEL ALBUM?
SIMON AND GARFUNKEL ??
US
© King Features Syndicate, Inc., 1969. World rights reserved.
BLAM
BLAM
THE END
MORT WALKER
3-9

WELL, TODAY'S THE DAY I WIN THE PING-PONG TOURNAMENT, BEETLE

FRANKLY, SARGE, I DON'T THINK YOU HAVE A CHANCE

LISTEN! I'M GOING TO WIN!
AREN'T I?

FRANKLY, AS A PING-PONG PLAYER, YOU STINK, SARGE
YOUR SERVE DOESN'T HAVE ANY SPIN ON IT
YOUR BACKHAND IS STRICTLY DEFENSIVE
AND YOU MOVE AROUND LIKE EACH FOOT IS IN A BUCKET OF CEMENT

YOU ONLY GOT TO THE FINALS BY PURE, DUMB LUCK
LUCK?!
© King Features Syndicate, Inc., 1969. World rights reserved
IT'S ALMOST TIME FOR THE TOURNAMENT TO START, BEETLE. WILL YOU WARM UP SARGE?
I JUST DID
THE END
3-16

BEETLE!
YOU WANT YOUR COFFEE NOW, SARGE?
IT'S 10:31
I KNOW. YOU WANTED YOUR COFFEE AT 10:30, DIDN'T YOU?
10:31 IS **NOT** 10:30!!

BEETLE, FOR ONCE IN YOUR LIFE, TRY TO DO SOMETHING RIGHT! IF A THING IS WORTH DOING AT ALL...
--IT'S WORTH DOING RIGHT
NOW, THIS COFFEE YOU'RE GOING AFTER IS FOR ME, RIGHT? IT'S NOT JUST FOR ANYBODY. AND IT OUGHT TO BE THE WAY I LIKE IT, NOT THE WAY I DON'T LIKE IT
RIGHT! THE WAY YOU LIKE IT
--AND FOUR SPOONFULS OF SUGAR. NOT TWO--NOT THREE--FOUR! CREAM, NOT MILK--AND NOT JUST OUT OF THE REFRIGERATOR. THAT MAKES THE COFFEE COOL TOO FAST. GOT ALL THAT SO FAR?
YEAH--YEAH--

WHAT WAS THAT ALL ABOUT ?
HE'S INCREDIBLE. 15 MINUTES TO TELL ME HOW HE LIKES HIS COFFEE!
HOLD IT!
NOW, AS TO THE TOASTED ENGLISH MUFFIN---
THE END
3-23
© King Features Syndicate, Inc., 1969. World rights reserved.

ZERO, TAKE OVER THIS JOB WHILE I GO TO THE WAREHOUSE

BOY! AM I GLAD I DON'T HAVE TO DO THIS DAY AFTER DAY
I WONDER WHAT COOKIE THINKS ABOUT ALL DAY?
WELL, I'M NOT GOING TO WASTE TIME! I'M GOING TO THINK ABOUT SOMETHING!
© King Features Syndicate, Inc., 1969. World rights reserved.

I WONDER WHAT COOKIE THINKS ABOUT ALL DAY?
4-6
MORT WALKER
THE END

AH! THERE'S A GOOD GOLF TOURNAMENT ON TODAY
IF HE SINKS THIS PUTT, HE'LL WIN $35,000!
I'M GLAD IT'S APRIL AND SARGE CAN'T COME IN RIGHT NOW AND SWITCH TO SOME FOOTBALL GAME

THERE GOES THE PUTT.....

I WANT TO WATCH FOOTBALL
BUT, SARGE, THE FOOTBALL SEASON IS OVER
CLICK
CLICK

WHO CARES ABOUT SEASONS! I WANTA WATCH FOOTBALL!!
BAM

THAT WON'T DO ANY GOOD, SARGE
FOOTBALL!! DURN BURN IT!! I WANT FOOTBALL!!
NAMATH PASSES INTO THE END ZONE AND IT'S ANOTHER TOUCHDOWN FOR THE JETS!
© King Features Syndicate, Inc., 1969. World rights reserved.
4-13
THE CHILLING PART OF IT IS HE DOESN'T SEE ANYTHING UNUSUAL ABOUT IT
MORT WALKER
THE END

WOW! LOOK AT HIM GO!
I DON'T BELIEVE IT!

HEY, BEETLE! HOW COME YOU'RE WORKING SO EAGERLY ?
BECAUSE I **LIKE** TO WORK

BEETLE SAID HE **LIKES** TO **WORK?!**
RACE YOU TO THE PSYCHIATRIST

SARGE SAID HE'D TEAR UP MY FURLOUGH IF HE HEARD ONE MORE GRIPE · FROM ME

I'LL SHOW HIM!
I'LL WORK LIKE A TIGER

AND SMILE SMILE SMILE
HE'S JUST LOOKING FOR AN EXCUSE TO TEAR UP MY FURLOUGH

WELL, I'M GOING TO DO AN EXTRA SPECIAL JOB TODAY
AND HE WON'T HEAR ONE LITTLE GRIPE FROM ME
HUH
I HEARD THAT DEEP SIGH, BEETLE!
MORT WALKER
4-20
THE END

WHAT'S THE NAME OF THAT SONG, BEETLE?
BETCHA CAN'T GUESS
IT'S SWEET SOMETHING!
"SWEET LEILANI"?
"SWEET LORRAINE"?
I KNOW IT'S NOT "SWEET GEORGIA BROWN"
I BETTER TELL YOU, SARGE...
NO! NO! NO! I'LL GET IT!
"SWEET SUE, JUST YOU"!

I GOTTA TELL YOU...
NO!
"SWEET BYE AND BYE"?
"SWEET DREAMS"?
"LET ME CALL YOU SWEETHEART"?
"MY SWEETIE FROM TAHITI"?
"NUTCRACKER SUITE"?
AREN'T YOU GOING TO TELL HIM, BEETLE?
YOU CAN TELL HIM

BUT I DON'T KNOW WHAT IT IS
WAIT TILL I'M ON THE BUS AND THEN TELL HIM I DON'T KNOW, EITHER
THE END
MORT WALKER
4-27

IS HE LEAVING FOR THE MEETING ALREADY? THE GENERAL ISN'T GOING TO SPEAK TILL 11:00
HE LIKES TO BE EARLY

GOSH! I FEEL I'M AT THE SCENE OF GREAT POWER
HERE'S WHERE THE GENERAL COMMUNICATES HIS MILITARY PHILOSOPHY
HERE'S WHERE THE BALL STARTS ROLLING

HARUMPH
HERE'S WHERE HE HARUMPHS

DRAT! I'VE COME AWAY WITHOUT MY NOTES!
LET ME GET THEM FOR YOU, SIR!
G-GOLLY! I'VE GOT GOOSE BUMPS ALL OVER LIKE WHEN I ENTERED GRANT'S TOMB
THIS IS **HIS** DESK! **HIS** MEMO PAD! **HIS** PENCIL!

TO THINK THAT I, A MERE LIEUTENANT, AM ACTUALLY SITTING IN THE VERY SPOT WHERE **HE** SITS WHEN **HE** MAKES DECISIONS!
YES
NO
THERE!
5-4
MORT WALKER
© King Features Syndicate, Inc., 1969. World rights reserved.
THE END

ONE LITTLE RAIN AND LOOK AT THIS PLACE!

IT TAKES A REAL FLEA-BRAIN TO SELECT A SPOT LIKE THIS TO CAMP IN
SHHH. SARGE MIGHT HEAR YOU

SO WHAT?! DO YOU THINK I'M AFRAID TO SPEAK MY OWN MIND?! I'LL SHOW YOU!

NICE GOING, SARGE! YOU'VE DONE IT AGAIN!
© King Features Syndicate, Inc., 1969. World rights reserved.

YOU'VE FOUND US ANOTHER GARDEN SPOT TO BIVOUAC IN!!

WITH LOTS OF GOOD FIREWOOD

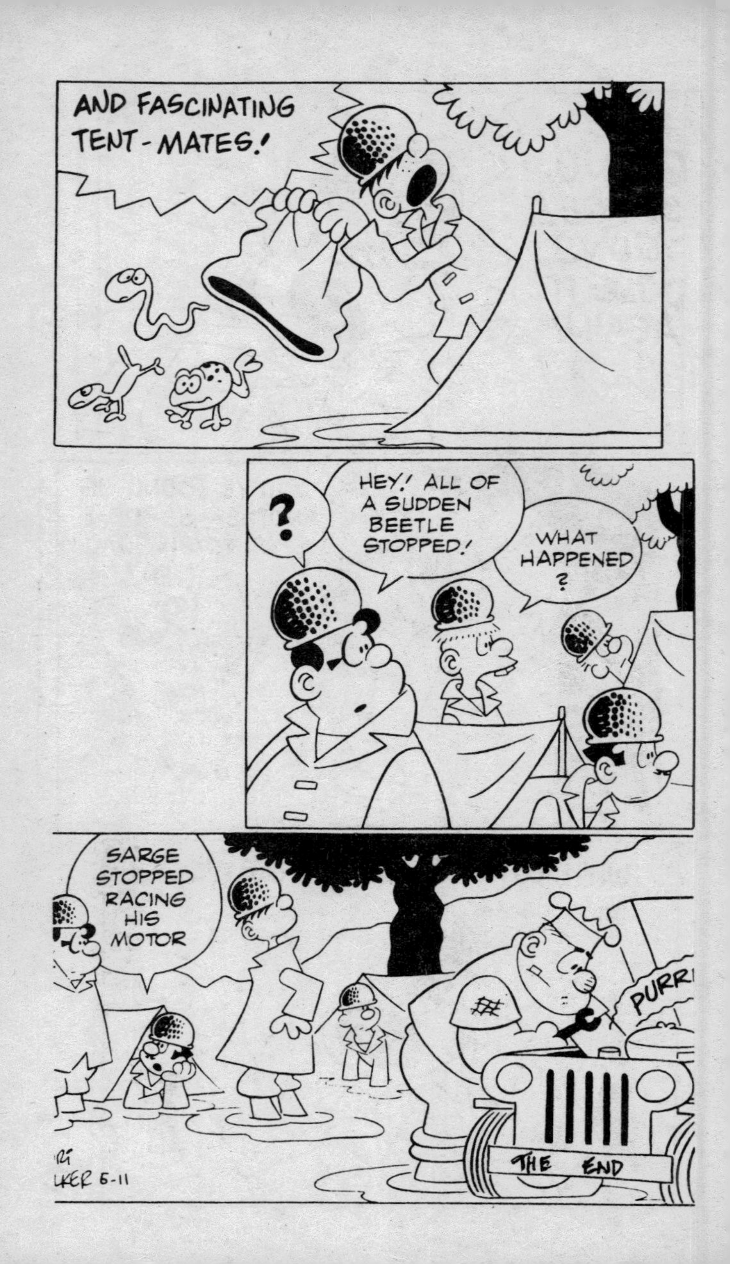
AND FASCINATING TENT-MATES!
?
HEY! ALL OF A SUDDEN BEETLE STOPPED!
WHAT HAPPENED ?
SARGE STOPPED RACING HIS MOTOR
PURR
THE END
LKER 5-11

BEETLE! STOP THAT WHISTLING !!

SORRY, BEETLE
THAT'S OKAY. YOU CAN'T HELP IT IF SARGE ALWAYS PICKS ON ME.

BLAST YOU, BEETLE!

BEETLE, YOU@*!!

WHAT IN THE WORLD ARE YOU BLAMING ME FOR NOW?!
I CAN'T SLEEP

HOW CAN YOU BLAME **ME** FOR **THAT?!** AM I SUPPOSED TO BE RESPONSIBLE FOR **EVERYTHING** THAT GOES WRONG AROUND HERE?!
I'M SORRY, BEETLE
US
I GUESS IT'S JUST A BAD HABIT I'VE FALLEN INTO
GEE!
WHAT WAS THAT ALL ABOUT? DID HE FIND OUT YOU HID HIS CLIPBOARD AND DUTY-ROSTER FILE BOX?
NAW, THEY'RE STILL TUCKED UNDER HIS MATTRESS
HIS **MATTRESS!**
MORT WALKER
5-18

WHO LEFT THIS WATER RUNNING?!
I GUESS BEETLE DID
THEY YELLED MAIL CALL AND HE JUST RAN
JERK!

HEY, SARGE! YOU KNOW THAT CONTEST THE PENTAGON HELD FOR EFFICIENCY IDEAS?!
YEAH

I WON FIRST PRIZE!!
THUNK

LUCKY YOU WERE ONLY HOLDING YOUR CANTEEN, SARGE
YOU SHOULD BE MORE CAREFUL HOW YOU TELL ME NEWS LIKE THAT, BEETLE

THE PENTAGON JUST ANNOUNCED THE WINNER OF THEIR EFFICIENCY AWARD...
...PVT. BEETLE BAILEY
CRASH
CRASH
CRASH!
5-25
CRASH!
CRASH
CRASH
CRASH
CRASH
CRASH
THE END

I DON'T FEEL LIKE GOING TO THE MESS HALL TONIGHT
I THINK I'LL STAY HERE AND WARM UP A CAN OF "C" RATIONS
IT'S BEEN A LONG TIME SINCE I HAD A NICE HOME-COOKED MEAL
CAN I BORROW A PENCIL, KILLER? I WANT TO WRITE MY MOTHER

WRITING HOME, BEETLE?
YEAH
© King Features Syndicate, Inc., 1969. World rights reserved.

WELL.. UH.. ASK YOUR MOM TO MAKE US SOME MORE OF THOSE LITTLE COOKIES SHE SENT YOU LAST CHRISTMAS
YOU MEAN HER MOLASSES SQUARES?

NO! NOT MOLASSES SQUARES. THE SMALL, ROUND, LIGHT-BROWN COOKIES COVERED WITH DIFFERENT-COLORED SUGAR CRYSTALS...
OH, YEAH-- WHAT DOES SHE CALL THEM?

YOU KNOW DARN WELL WHAT SHE CALLS THEM! YOU JUST LIKE TO HEAR ME SAY IT!
FORGET IT, THEN
DON'T GET SORE, BEETLE. JUST ASK YOUR MOM TO SEND SOME OF HER --UH--UH--
6-1
..DINKY TWINKLY SPRINKLES
OH, THOSE
THE END

BEAUTIFUL DAY, SIR
HUNH.

ATTENTION!

HERE HE COMES. I HOPE HE'S IN A GOOD MOOD TODAY

GOOD MORNING, SIR
MPHM

I'VE FINISHED THAT REPORT, GENERAL
MMRP

SIR, DID YOU WANT TO DICTATE NOW?
GETOUTHERE

GOOD NIGHT, SIR
GNNYT.
BOY! WHAT A GROUCH HE'S BEEN TODAY!
I FEEL SORRY FOR SOMEONE WHEN HE GETS HOME!
© King Features Syndicate, Inc., 1969. World rights reserved.
6-8
♪♪ HELLO, DEAR ♪♪
THE END
Mort WALKER

GRRRR
HEH HEH HEH
BEETLE SURE ENJOYS MAKING SARGE MAD
WELL, HE'S REALLY ENJOYING HIMSELF NOW
BUT I'M AFRAID SARGE WILL HAVE THE LAST LAUGH

LOOK AT SARGE DIG IN! HE'S SORE BECAUSE BEETLE STRUCK HIM OUT LAST TIME UP

2
WHAP
© King Features Syndicate, Inc., 1969. World rights reserved.

GOL-LEE!!
SARGE HIT IT OVER THE WATER TOWER
THAT'S GOTTA BE A RECORD HOME RUN!

THIS IS FOR THE RECORD BOOK, SARGE. WE WANT TO GET THE PRECISE FOOTAGE OF YOUR HOMER

I REALLY GOT THE WOOD INTO THAT ONE! I HOPE THEY FIND THE EXACT SPOT WHERE THE BALL LANDED
MORT WALKER
6-15

2
THE END

NOW WE'LL TAKE UP THE FRAMMIS JNG ON RANG Z
Z

THE RAMPJG IS LVTD ONNA BRNSTL **BMM!**

SURE IS HARD TO SLEEP WITH ALL THAT TALKING

GOOD GOLLY! WHAT A BORING LECTURE! I GOTTA SNEAK OUT OF HERE

GRADUALLY SINK DOWN.. CRAWL ALONG THE BACK WALL... SLITHER OUT THE SIDE DOOR

CRASH!
NOW, WAIT A MINUTE, SARGE..
OW!!
POW
SCRAPE!

6-22
I MUST BRUSH UP ON MY SLINKING, CRAWLING AND SLITHERING
MORT WALKER
THE END

AHA! CAUGHT YOU GOOFING OFF!

I DECIDED I'D RATHER NOT HAVE YOU ORGANIZE MY TIME, SARGE
I'LL NOT ONLY ORGANIZE YOUR TIME, I'LL ORGANIZE YOUR FACE!

HOLD IT! I THINK A CONDEMNED MAN SHOULD BE ALLOWED A FINAL STATEMENT

NOW, CONSIDER FOR A MOMENT THAT MOST OF MANKIND'S PROBLEMS COME FROM TOO MUCH ORGANIZATION

LOOK AT THE PRODUCTION FIGURES IN CUBA AFTER CASTRO BEGAN REGIMENTING EVERYONE

AND LOOK WHAT HAPPENED TO ENGLAND WHEN IT TRIED TO MAINTAIN A WORLD EMPIRE

OF COURSE YOU KNOW HOW HITLER FARED WHEN HE IMPOSED HIS BRAND OF CULTURE ON EUROPE

DON'T MOVE. I'LL GO GET THE CAPTAIN

YOU GOTTA SEE THIS, SIR--- A DOCUMENTED GOOF-OFF!
MORT WALKER
6-29
THE END

C'MON, ZERO, DO IT AGAIN
OKAY
ZERO IS WIGGLING HIS EARS!
VERY FEW PEOPLE CAN DO THAT

GOLLY, THIS PAINT IS GUMMY
ZERO, SHAKE THIS PAINT UP FOR ME, WILL YOU?
TOSS IT DOWN
PAIN
PAINT

© King Features Syndicate, Inc., 1969. World rights reserved
PAINT

PAINT

PAINT

HERE, BEETLE
PAINT

BOY, THAT REALLY WAKES A GUY UP
YEAH, BUT THE PAINT IS STILL ASLEEP!
7-6
THE END

HOW'S THE STEAK, SARGE ?

NEVER MIND. I'LL ASK SOMEONE ELSE

HOW'S THE STEAK, BEETLE ?

NOBODY EVER ANSWERS AROUND THIS PLACE
THE END
MORT WALKER 7-20

WHERE'S SARGE?
I DON'T KNOW, SIR. HE WAS WITH BEETLE

BEETLE! WHERE'S SARGE?
ISN'T HE BACK, SIR? HE WAS GOING TO EXPLORE A NEW ROUTE THROUGH THE GORGE

I TOLD HIM HE'D HAVE A HARD TIME. THAT AREA IS LIKE A BIG JUNGLE

SARGE IS TWO HOURS OVERDUE. I HOPE HE'S NOT LOST IN THOSE WOODS
DON'T WORRY, SIR

WHEN HE SMELLS DINNER COOKING HE'LL JUST FOLLOW HIS NOSE

SEE? HE'S MAGNETICALLY DRAWN TO GOOD FOOD

MORT WALKER
BURGER
IN
THE END

Z
JULIUS!
READY TO GO, SIR?
YOU KNOCKED YOUR HAT OFF
BONK!
US

OOPS! I'M SORRY, SIR
OW!

GOSH! I'M REALLY BUTTERFINGERED TODAY!

I DIDN'T GET MUCH SLEEP LAST NIGHT. MY NERVES ARE SHOT

DO YOU EVER HAVE DAYS WHEN YOU FEEL UNCOORDINATED LIKE THIS, GENERAL?

GENERAL...
© King Features Syndicate, Inc., 1969. World rights reserved.
MORT WALKER
8-3

THE END

UMMMM

WELL, SO FAR
THE CAMP IS
RUNNING VERY
SMOOTHLY

OF COURSE, NO
ONE IS UP YET

OH, WHAT A BEAUTIFUL MORN-ING

SUNNY SKIES, TEMPERATURE IN THE SEVENTIES, SOFT, BALMY BREEZES...

THIS IS **MY** KIND OF DAY
I'M NOT GOING TO LET **ANYONE** OR **ANYTHING** RUIN IT FOR ME

ROLL CALL!

NOW WHAT?
8-10

Z
Z
Z Z
Z
THE END

TABLE CLEAN---
SUGAR BOWL FULL--
SALT AND PEPPER...
KETCHUP---

GOTTA MAKE
SURE EVERYTHING
IS IN GOOD SHAPE
FOR THE GENERAL

HOLD
IT!

THE GENERAL'S COMING TO DINNER. PUT ON A SHIRT AND LOOK DECENT
BUT IT'S **HOT** COOKING OVER THIS STOVE
IT GOT OVER 110° ON THE DRILL FIELD YESTERDAY, BUT YOU DIDN'T SEE **ME** TAKE OFF MY SHIRT
WELL, IT MUST GET HOTTER THAN THAT IN HERE
OH, YEAH?! WHERE'S A THERMOMETER?

WHAT DOES IT SAY?
150°

150° ?!
© King Features Syndicate, Inc., 1969. World rights reserved.
MORT WALKER

SIT RIGHT OVER HERE, SIR
NOW WHAT ?
THE END

EVERYONE TAKE A DEEP BREATH
NOW EXHALE.. I HAVE TWO MORE MEN WHO HAVE TO FIT IN THERE
I FINALLY GOT THEM ALL IN, SIR
GOOD. NOW WHERE'S BEETLE WITH THE JEEP?

LET'S SEE... HOW SHOULD WE DO THIS?
WE HAVE A MAJOR, A CAPTAIN, A LIEUTENANT, A SERGEANT AND A DRIVER
THAT'S **FIVE** AND WE ONLY HAVE ROOM FOR **FOUR!** ONE OF US HAS TO RIDE IN THE TRUCK WITH THE MEN
OBVIOUSLY, THAT WILL BE SARGE
© King Features Syndicate, Inc., 1969. World rights reserved
WHY OBVIOUSLY SARGE? THERE'S NO ROOM FOR **ME** IN THE TRUCK, BUT **YOU** MIGHT SQUEEZE IN, SIR
I **HAPPEN** TO BE AN **OFFICER**, AND YOU **HAPPEN** TO BE THE ONLY ONE HERE WHO **ISN'T!**

WHAT ABOUT BEETLE?!
HE'S THE DRIVER!
COULDN'T ONE OF US DRIVE?
I ALWAYS HAVE A DRIVER
MAYBE IF WE ALL STOOD, WE MIGHT--
ME? A MAJOR, STAND ALL THE WAY BACK TO CAMP?!
I'VE GOT AN IDEA, SIR
THAT'S IT, SIR-- YOU WORK THE PEDALS AND I'LL STEER
THIS IS KINDA SLOW
THAT'S OKAY. DOING THINGS THE PROPER ARMY WAY IS WHAT COUNTS
MORT WALKER
THE END
8-24

IT'S PROBABLY TIME TO GET UP

ON THE OTHER HAND, I GET THE FEELING THIS WOULD BE A GOOD DAY TO STAY IN BED

BEETLE,
SGT. SNORKEL
WANTS TO
SEE YOU

BEETLE!
CAPT. SCABBARD
WANTS TO
SEE YOU!

HEY, BEETLE!
MAJOR GREENBRASS
WANTS TO SEE YOU

BEETLE! COL. KARP WANTS TO SEE YOU
© King Features Syndicate, Inc., 1969. World rights reserved.

BEETLE! GEN. HALFTRACK WANTS TO SEE YOU!

BOY! A GOOD GOOF-UP SURE GETS THROUGH CHANNELS FAST
MORT WALKER
THE END
8-31

GOOD. EVERYONE'S ASLEEP. I MIGHT AS WELL PUT OUT THE LIGHTS
Z
Z
Z
Z
Z

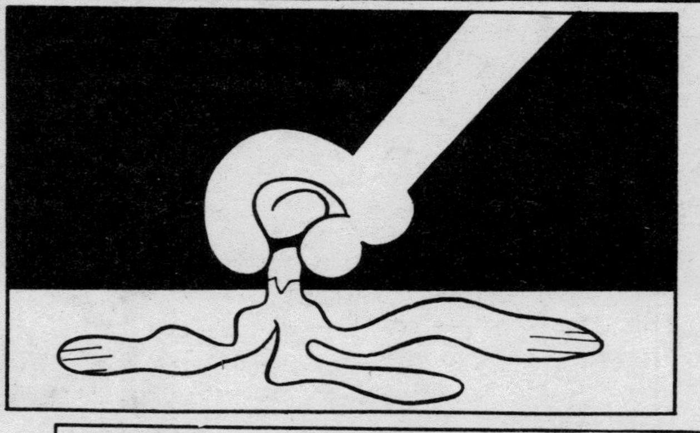

Z
Z
Z
Z

SWISH!

PLOM!

ALL RIGHT! WHO PUT THAT BANANA PEEL FOR ME TO SLIP ON?

WON'T CONFESS, HUH? WELL, NEVER MIND! I'LL FIND OUT WHICH ONE OF YOU DID IT!!
MORT WALKER
Z
Z
Z
Z
Z
Z
Z
9-7
ALL I HAVE TO DO IS CHECK FOR STIFLED LAUGHTER
Z
THE END

LAST TIME, WE FOUND OURSELVES IN THE MIDDLE OF A BALL GAME BETWEEN "C" AND "D" COMPANIES
IT WON'T HAPPEN AGAIN

I'LL MAKE SURE IT DOESN'T HAPPEN AGAIN

IT'S THE GENERAL FOR YOU, SIR

THE OLD FOLKS ARE HAVING AN OUTING ON THE DRILL FIELD TODAY. BE SURE NO ONE BOTHERS THEM.
YES, SIR
ZERO, GO SEE WHO THAT IS
GUAR
GUAR

I'M A SENIOR CITIZEN
GUARD

WELL, WHO WAS IT?
GUARD
© King Features Syndicate, Inc., 1969 World rights reserved

SOME SPANISH GUY NAMED CITIZEN
GUARD
MORT WALKER
9-14
THE END

LET'S SEE IF WE CAN FIND SOMEONE TO HELP SARGE GET CAUGHT UP ON HIS PAPER WORK
YES, SIR
OH, PLATO! JUST THE MAN I WAS LOOKING FOR TO DO SOME TYPING
I KNEW I SHOULDN'T PASS BY HERE
ANYONE SEE ZERO?

WOOF! FINISHED AT LAST! I NEED A DRINK OF WATER!

HOW ABOUT THAT? NOT A SINGLE MISTAKE!

THAT'S **GREAT,** ZERO! **FABULOUS!** THIS IS A TREMENDOUS BREAKTHROUGH! I ALWAYS KNEW THERE WAS SOMETHING IN THAT OLD BEAN!

ZERO, I DON'T OFTEN DO THIS, BUT TOMORROW MORNING THERE'LL BE SOMETHING **NICE** UNDER YOUR **PILLOW!**
© King Features Syndicate, Inc., 1969. World rights reserved.
MORT WALKER

I WONDER WHAT THAT WAS ALL ABOUT?
AH!
9-21
THE END

HMMM

Dear Mom and Dad,
How are you?
I am fine.

IT'S THE SAME PROBLEM EVERY WEEK. I GET THIS FAR AND RUN OUT OF INFORMATION

WRITING YOUR WEEKLY LETTER HOME, BEETLE?
YEAH-- IT SURE IS HARD FOR ME TO THINK OF THINGS TO SAY

TELL YOUR FOLKS ABOUT THE THREE-ALARM NIGHT CLUB FIRE WE SAW IN HURLEYBURG

AND THE TWO-HEADED TREE TOAD I FOUND ON BIVOUAC
HOW ABOUT MENTIONING SARGE'S NEW TATTOO?

GEN. HALFTRACK FINALLY BROKE A HUNDRED
ROCKY BOUGHT A NEW GUITAR
SARGE WON THE PIZZA-EATING CONTEST
LT. FUZZ HAS THE MUMPS
COL. GREENBRASS GOT A TOUPEE
OTTO BIT THE MAILMAN

GEE, THANKS! YOU GUYS HAVE GIVEN ME **LOTS** TO WRITE HOME ABOUT!
MORT WALKER

BEETLE SAW A THREE-ALARM FIRE? WHAT ELSE DOES HE SAY?
"MORE NEWS NEXT WEEK"
9-28

THE END

DARN! THIS SCREWDRIVER IS TOO BIG. I GOTTA GO GET THE OTHER ONE

DARN!

WELL, I DON'T CARE WHAT SARGE SAYS, THAT PENCIL SHARPENER JUST CAN'T BE FIXED

BEETLE

I TOLD YOU TO TIGHTEN THOSE SCREWS ON THAT PENCIL SHARPENER
I TRIED TO, SARGE, BUT THESE SCREW-DRIVERS ARE TOO BIG

WELL, THEN, YOU NINNY... IMPROVISE, IMPROVISE!!

TRY USING A COIN OR A KNIFE! LOOK AROUND FOR SOMETHING TO TURN THOSE SCREWS!

I'LL BE BACK IN TEN MINUTES, AND I WANT TO SEE THAT JOB **DONE**!
STOP

SCREEEECH!
CRASH
TINKLE
THE END
10-5

HELLO, TINA?
YEAH, THIS IS PLATO

I WAS WONDERING ABOUT TOMORROW NIGHT...
I DIDN'T? --OH-- I THOUGHT I MENTIONED IT LAST WEEK..

YEAH--- UH HUH-- --MMM---
203
QU3-9775

--WELL-- MAYBE NEXT WEEK?--- UH HUH--- UH HUH---
203
QU3-9775

--OKAY---YEAH, I UNDERSTAND--SEE YOU AROUND--YEAH, ME TOO---`BYE
Of all liars, the smoothest and most convincing is

Of all liars, the smoothest and most convincing is memory. Doesn't it follow then, that no man has a good enough memory to be a successful liar?

Of all liars, the smoothest and most convincing is memory. Doesn't it follow then, that no man has a good enough memory to be a successful liar? Surely, too morality is moral only when it is voluntary. Truth, Beauty, Freedom! – Should one not concern oneself with these to the exclusion of all else? For the silence of the uncommitted is deafening. And are not the cruelest lies told
10-12

ence? The liberty to do as one chooses,
love, create, in peace and contentment, –
the dictates of conscience – these are
worth pursuing, worth fighting for. To find
love, to woo it and to win it, secure in the
that final and complete. For love
all growths. In the end,
ONCE HE GETS GOING ON AN IDEA, HE DOESN'T LIKE TO STOP
THE END
MORT WALKER

AND THAT'S JUST A LIST OF THINGS HE DID **TODAY,** SIR

I THINK BEETLE SHOULD BE GIVEN A LITTLE TALKING-TO, SARGE
JUST WHAT I THOUGHT, SIR

IN FACT, I THOUGHT I'D DO **VERY** LITTLE TALKING

IF YOU EVER DO THAT AGAIN, BEETLE, I'LL REALLY GIVE YOU A GOING-OVER!!!

UNDERSTAND ?!
ALL RIGHT!!

I HOPE YOU WEREN'T TOO ROUGH ON BEETLE, SARGE
HE WAS SMILING WHEN I LEFT HIM, SIR
THE END
10-19

ROCKY, IS THAT THING LOADED?
I DON'T KNOW. I'LL SEE

POW

QUICK! SARGE IS AFTER ME! WHERE CAN I HIDE?!
MY FAVORITE HIDING PLACE IS ANY EMPTY TRASH CAN

WHERE IS HE?! WHERE IS HE?!
THANKS, BEETLE

I'LL TEAR HIM APART!
ZIP!

I'LL BET HE'S IN ONE OF THESE CANS!!

BEETLE!! I'M NOT AFTER YOU! WHAT ARE YOU HIDING FOR ?
MY MIND SAID "RELAX! RELAX! HE'S NOT CHASING YOU!"
MORT WALKER
10-26

BUT MY LEGS WOULDN'T BELIEVE IT
© King Features Syndicate, Inc., 1969. World rights reserved.
THE END

WHEN ARE WE GOING TO GET TO THAT TOWN, SARGE?

WHERE ARE WE **NOW**, BEETLE?
I THOUGHT **YOU** KNEW!

STUPID
JERK!
MAYBE THAT KID KNOWS SOMETHING

HEY, KID, WE SEEM TO BE A LITTLE LOST..DO YOU KNOW HOW TO GET TO...UH... LET'S SEE....WHAT'S THE NAME OF---
GET DOWN HERE, BEETLE, AND LET ME UP!
WHY DON'T YOU JUST SHOUT UP TO ME WHAT YOU WANT TO SAY TO THE KID, SARGE ---I COULD HAVE--
OH, JUST GET OUT OF THE !! WAY, BEETLE!
NOW LISTEN CAREFULLY, KID...
I DON'T LIKE YOU. I'LL ONLY TALK TO THE OTHER MAN
© King Features Syndicate, Inc., 1969. World rights reserved

GO ON UP, BEETLE. HE'LL ONLY TALK TO **YOU**
HE'S A SMART KID
MORT WALKER
NOW, WHAT'S THE NAME OF THAT PLACE WE WANT, SARGE?
???? **BLAST** IT! NOW **I'VE** FORGOTTEN IT!!.... @✿!!!

SOMETHING CORNERS... OH, YEAH... THAT'S IT! **FOUR CORNERS!** ASK HIM, BEETLE!
NEVER MIND. HE'S GONE
THE END
11-2

SARGE LOVES "PX ROZ"

WAIT'LL I GET MY HANDS ON THE @✱ WHO..
SARGE LOVES "PX ROZ"

I'LL..
SARGE, THAT'S NO WAY FOR A GROWN MAN TO ACT

THE NEXT TIME YOU FEEL LIKE LOSING YOUR TEMPER, TRY COUNTING TO TEN
YES, SIR

IT WILL HELP YOU...
THOK!

ONE! TWO! THREE!

FOUR! FIVE! SIX!

SEVEN! EIGHT! NINE!

YOU'RE RIGHT, CHAPLAIN! THAT DID HELP!
THE END
MORT WALKER 11-9

SHHH

BE QUIET. THEY'RE HAVING A MEETING
I DON'T HEAR ANYTHING
CONFERENCE ROOM

THAT'S BECAUSE THE GENERAL ALWAYS STARTS BY FIXING EVERYONE WITH A DARK GLOWER

MINUTES OF THE LAST MEETING, SIR.
DO WE HAVE TO? OH, VERY WELL -- PROCEED

--then Col. Greenbrass gave the officers' club treasury report, months April to August, except for June, which was lost--

..Lt. Fuzz then said he didn't think so. Lt. Algae said he did think so. Lt. Fuzz said he didn't think so...

--major Whinny announced that the ladies' canasta and chitchat group would hold its--

--after the vote, Lt. Fuzz jumped up and began stamping his foot. Captain Scabbard said to stop having tantrums. Lt. Fuzz said he wasn't having--

THE GENERAL HAS A LOW THRESHOLD FOR BOREDOM, DOESN'T HE?
Z
11-16
Mort WALKER
© King Features Syndicate, Inc., 1969. World rights reserved.

THE END

LOOK OUT!

YOU'RE ALWAYS IN THE WAY, BEETLE!

I'D BETTER LEAVE, THEN
COME BACK HERE!!

FIND ME SOME GOOD, STRONG STRING, BEETLE
WHAT DO YOU WANT IT FOR?

LISTEN! YOU, A PRIVATE, DO NOT ASK ME, A SERGEANT, WHAT I WANT ANYTHING FOR!!

UNDERSTAND?! IF I WANT IT, I WANT IT!! GOT IT?!! AND IF I TELL YOU TO GET IT, GET IT!! GOT IT?!! NOW, GET GOING!!
WHEW!

I FINALLY FOUND SOME STRING, SARGE
FINE, FINE! NOW, WITH ALL THAT FUSS, I FORGOT WHAT I WANTED IT FOR!
MORT WALKER

WHAT?! YOU SEND ME ALL OVER THE STUPID CAMP HUNTING FOR A STUPID...

UNTIL I REMEMBER WHY I WANTED IT, THAT WILL DO!
© King Features Syndicate, Inc., 1969. World rights reserved.
11-23
THE END

WHY ARE YOU KNOCKING YOURSELF OUT, BEETLE?

I'VE DISCOVERED THAT DOING A GOOD CAMOUFLAGE JOB HAS ITS ADVANTAGES
YOU FIND IT MAKES SARGE HAPPY?

NO, BUT IT MAKES ME HAPPY WHEN SARGE CAN'T FIND **ME**
I **LIKE** HIS THINKING

WHERE ARE THE MEN, SARGE?
OVER IN THE CAMOUFLAGE AREA GETTING READY FOR ME TO INSPECT THEM

THIS LOOKS LIKE A GOOD SPOT FOR OUR NATURE STUDY, GIRLS

WHAT KIND OF A BUSH IS THIS, MISS ROOT?
DOES IT HAVE NEEDLES?

NO...PINCHERS!

WHAT KIND OF A TREE **WHISTLES,** MISS ROOT ?

AND WHAT KIND OF A SHRUB SAYS, "HELLO, BABY"?
© King Features Syndicate, Inc., 1969. World rights reserved.

I DON'T CARE IF YOU **ARE** A CHRISTMAS TREE...KEEP YOUR BRANCHES TO YOURSELF
COME, GIRLS! I WANT TO GET BACK TO THE SCHOOL RIGHT AWAY!!
MORT WALKER 11-30

SHE JUST KEEPS SAYING SHE WANTS TO DO A LITTLE MORE RESEARCH
THE END

WELL, HOW DO YOU THINK IT WENT, SIR?
HOW DO I THINK **WHAT** WENT?
HOW DO YOU THINK THE MANEUVER WENT?
BETTER THAN USUAL
NO COWS WERE SHOT, NO GIRLS WERE REPORTED MISSING, AND MOST OF THE MOUNTAINS ARE STILL THERE

AS A REWARD FOR A SUCCESSFUL MANEUVER, THE GENERAL IS GIVING US THE WEEKEND OFF.

DIS-
MISSED!

YIPPEE!! YIPPEE! YIPPEE!!

HIPPEE!!
YIPPEE!!
CLAP
CLAP

YIPPEE
MORT WALKER
THE END
12-7

WHEN ARE THOSE GUYS GOING TO GROW UP?!

THE GENERAL SAID NO BALL PLAYING ON THE LAWN!
THAT'S A STUPID ORDER

LISTEN! I DON'T CARE HOW STUPID THE GENERAL'S ORDERS ARE! YOU'LL OBEY EVERY STUPID ONE OF THEM!!
US

SERGEANT! I WANT TO SPEAK TO YOU!!

SARGE IS LIKE A LITTLE BOY WHEN HE GETS CAUGHT DOING SOMETHING WRONG

NOTICE HOW HE SHUFFLES HIS FEET AND LOOKS INNOCENT

LOOK AT HIM PLEAD AND PROMISE HE'LL DO BETTER--- JUST LIKE A LITTLE BOY
US

HA HA
HEE HEE

BEETLE'S LIKE A LITTLE BABY WHEN HE GETS CAUGHT DOING SOMETHING WRONG
THE END
© King Features Syndicate, Inc., 1969. World rights reserved.
12-21

PHWEET

ROLL CALL

GEE, IT SURE GOT QUIET ALL OF A SUDDEN
MUST BE TIME TO GET UP

FOR MISSING ROLL CALL TODAY YOU CAN WORK AN HOUR ON THE GARBAGE CANS!
YOU DIDN'T BLOW YOUR WHISTLE FOR ROLL CALL
I BLEW MY WHISTLE, I YELLED, I EVEN KNOCKED ON THE WINDOW.. YOU WERE ASLEEP!
ANYWAY, I CAN'T WORK AN HOUR. I'M ON THE BASKETBALL TEAM
TOUGH

BUT I JUST WASHED THOSE GARBAGE CANS YESTERDAY
WASH 'EM AGAIN!

THE DOCTOR TOLD ME NOT TO GET THIS CUT WET
THAT WAS FOUR MONTHS AGO
LOOK! YOUR HOUR DOESN'T START UNTIL YOU BEGIN WORKING!!
MORT WALKER
I THINK EVERY PERIOD OF PUNISHMENT SHOULD ALLOW SOME TIME TO TRY AND GET OUT OF IT
© King Features Syndicate, Inc., 1968. World rights reserved.
1-7

THE END

AHEM!
NOW WHAT?
I'M THROUGH WITH THE FLOOR NOW, SARGE. CAN I GO TO THE PX FOR A MINUTE ?
NO!
WELL, IT DOESN'T HURT TO ASK

I'LL BE BACK IN ABOUT AN HOUR. IF THE GENERAL CALLS, TAKE THE MESSAGE!
HUH?... OH.. OKAY
?
HOW DO YOU GET AWAY WITH THAT?
PSYCHOLOGY! YOU GOTTA BE AGGRESSIVE! CATCH HIM OFF GUARD.. AND LEAVE BEFORE HE RECOVERS
I'LL BE DARNED! I NEVER KNEW IT WAS SO EASY!
MORT WALKER

THAT COSMO IS SURE A SMART OPERATOR
I WON'T BE BACK! FORWARD MY PAY CHECKS TO MY FOLKS' HOUSE IN ELM CITY
I DON'T THINK I LEFT QUICK ENOUGH
THE END
© King Features Syndicate, Inc., 1968. World rights reserved.
1/14

HE'S OUT IN THE CLEAR!
THERE GOES THE PASS!!
GO! GO!
OH-OH! HE BOBBLED IT!
YOU BIG JERK
NOW HERE'S THAT PLAY AGAIN.....
CLICK
IT WAS BAD ENOUGH THE FIRST TIME!

HEY! DON'T MESS WITH THAT PRACTICE MINE!
WE'RE BEING CAREFUL
YEAH! WE'RE BEING **VERY** CAREFUL NOT TO TOUCH TH...
FOOM

VIDEO TAPE REPLAY
YEAH! WE'RE BEING **VERY** CAREFUL NOT TO TOUCH TH...

VIDEO TAPE REPLAY
FOOM

I THINK I'M READY FOR THE END OF THE FOOTBALL SEASON
SWEET HOME
MORT WALKER

THE END

AHHHH
I'LL BE OUT ALL AFTERNOON
EXCUSE ME, SIR. YOU HAVE A VISITOR

GENERAL GREENBRASS! THIS IS A SURPRISE, SIR!
HIYA, HALFTRACK!

HOW'S THE WEATHER UP WHERE YOU ARE?
LOUSY! SNOW! ICE! 10° BELOW!

HOW'S EVERYTHING GOING HERE?
JUST FINE, SIR

BY THE WAY, IS THIS AN OFFICIAL VISIT?
IT SURE IS, HALFTRACK
US
US

IT WAS A LONG WAY TO COME, BUT I DID WANT TO ASK YOU HOW THINGS WERE GOING
MORT WALKER
© King Features Syndicate, Inc. 1968 World rights reserved.
1-28

WHY DIDN'T YOU JUST TELEPHONE?
THE END

LET'S GO!
WHERE ARE WE GOING TODAY?
TODAY WE'RE GOING TO HIKE UP BLISTER PEAK
BLISTER PEAK?!
THIS IS CRUEL AND INHUMAN!
I'LL WRITE MY CONGRESS-MAN!
CAN I BORROW YOUR PEN?
WHEN WE GET BACK

SARGE, I'M TIRED!
DO WE HAVE TO CLIMB ALL THE WAY TO THE TOP?
WHY ?
"B" COMPANY DOESN'T HAVE TO DO IT
THIS ISN'T FAIR

HOW MUCH LONGER ?
I DON'T THINK I CAN MAKE IT
I'M GOING TO FAINT

LOOK, BEETLE! WE'RE HERE! YOU MADE IT!!

WELL, FINALLY!
I'M SURE GLAD THE GRIPING IS OVER. YOU MUST BE THE ARMY'S ALL-TIME GRIPE CHAMP
OKAY, MEN! LET'S MOVE OUT!
© King Features Syndicate, Inc., 1968 World rights reserved
2-4
HOW LONG BEFORE WE GET TO THE BOTTOM?
MY BIG TOE HAS A CRAMP
THERE'S A STONE IN MY SOCK
WHEW!
MORT WALKER
THE END

DUST!
BEETLE!
BUT I ALREADY DUSTED THAT SHELF
THEN DUST IT AGAIN AND AGAIN AND AGAIN
AND WHEN YOU THINK YOU REALLY HAVE IT DUSTED, LET ME KNOW!

THAT'S NOT **ALL** I'LL LET HIM KNOW!

BEETLE, DID I SAY YOU COULD GO OUT OF THE OFFICE?
I'M JUST GOING OUT TO PUT THIS IN THE SUGGESTION BOX
WHY DON'T YOU SAVE A FEW STEPS AND JUST GIVE IT TO ME?
NAW, THAT'S OKAY
BUT I'M THE ONE WHO OPENS THE BOX AND READS THEM!
I'D STILL RATHER PUT IT IN THE BOX

DID YOU SIGN IT?
OF COURSE NOT!
GIVE ME THAT!!
TOO LATE!! HEE HEE! I DISGUISED MY WRITING TOO!
SUGGESTIO
GUESS WHAT! YOURS WAS THE ONLY SUGGESTION THIS WEEK
MORT WALKER
2-25
THE END

OW
IT'S ALL THAT STUPID SNORKEL'S FAULT FOR HAVING SUCH A LARGE DESK!

I DON'T SEE WHY A MERE SERGEANT SHOULD HAVE A LARGER DESK THAN A LIEUTENANT!
A **WHOLE INCH** LARGER!
NOT ONLY THAT, BUT HE CAME IN LATER THAN **I** DID YESTERDAY
HE DIDN'T REACH THE TOP STEP BEFORE I HAD MY HAT HUNG UP
AND IT'S POSITIVELY INSUBORDINATE THE WAY HE LETS HIS STOMACH GROWL AT ME

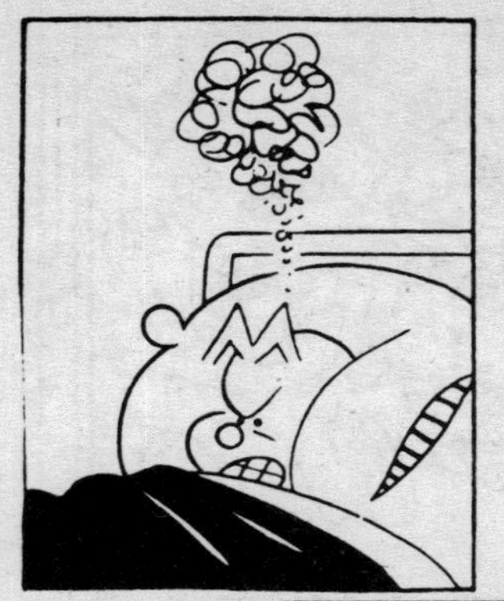

AND NOW. HE'S RUINING MY SLEEP!

THE ONLY WAY TO GET THIS OFF MY MIND IS TO MAKE A LIST OF MY GRIPES AND GIVE THEM TO HIM THE FIRST THING IN THE MORNING

SERGEANT!
LIEUTENANT!
MORT WALKER
3-3
THE END

THEY SURE ARE HAPPY TO GET PASSES
SMAK

TAXI

TAXI
SLURP
SLURP

© King Features Syndicate, Inc., 1968. World rights reserved.
SMAK
CAMP SWAM
WHAT'S WRONG WITH THEM?
AFTER A NIGHT IN TOWN IT TAKES THEM A WEEK TO UN-PUCKER!
MORT WALKER
3-10
THE END

I'LL BE DARNED! I THINK A WHOLE FILE IS MISSING!
A FILE **COULDN'T** BE MISSING. WE PROBABLY SHIPPED THE MEN OUT
I KNEW **YOU'D** REMEMBER, SIR
YES...AHEM! COFF! WELL THEY MUST BE AROUND HERE SOMEPLACE! COFF!
US
US
US

WHAT IF THE PENTAGON FINDS OUT THAT WE LOST TRACK OF A HUNDRED MEN, SIR?
ONCE AND FOR ALL.. THEY ARE NOT LOST!!
© King Features Syndicate, Inc. 1968 World rights reserved
THEY'RE AROUND HERE SOMEWHERE!
USE YOUR HEAD! YOU CAN'T JUST LOSE A HUNDRED MEN, NOW, CAN YOU?
RIDICULOUS!

I'LL ADMIT WE'VE TEMPORARILY MISPLACED THEIR RECORDS... BUT ONLY TEMPORARILY, MIND YOU
JUST TILL THEY'RE FOUND
WHAT EVERYONE MUST REALIZE IS, THE ARMY NEVER LOSES **ANYONE!**
EVEN IF THEY'RE **LOST!**

IF YOU DON'T SAY ANYTHING, MAYBE NO ONE WILL NOTICE
MORT WALKER
3-24
THE END

THE ONLY WAY TO DO THIS IS ONE AT A TIME
SIGH

STOP SLOUCHING, BEETLE!
DARN IT, SARGE! YOU'RE ALWAYS CRITICIZING!
CAN'T YOU EVER FIND ANYTHING GOOD TO SAY?
WELL, I DO ADMIRE THE WAY YOU PEEL A POTATO. YES, SIR, NOBODY PRODUCES A LONGER, THINNER PEEL THAN YOU DO
AND WHEN IT COMES TO REMOVING THE EYES, YOU HAVE NO PEER! YOU'RE THE MASTER!

BUT THE **GRACE** OF THE WHOLE OPERATION! THAT'S WHERE YOU **EXCEL!** THE FLUID MOVEMENT OF THE FINGERS! THE PRECISION TURNING OF THE WRIST!... PURE ART!

YOU SHOULD GO DOWN IN HISTORY AS ONE OF THE ALL-TIME GREAT POTATO PEELERS IN MY HUMBLE OPINION!

I GUESS ANYONE WHO OVERDOES CRITICISM TENDS TO OVERDO PRAISE
3-31
THE END

IT WON'T HURT TO ASK HIM AGAIN
CAN I BE YOUR TYPIST, SARGE?
NO, ZERO. YOU CAN'T SPELL ANY BETTER THAN I CAN
CLICK
CLICK
GEE, THAT WAS NICE OF HIM TO SAY THAT

All EM with mos 16
or CV. occ. 044.21
report to S-2
1900 hrs.
C.O.
I DON'T KNOW WHY SARGE WON'T LET ME BE HIS SECRETARY
MY LETTERS MAKE AS MUCH SENSE AS THIS!
IF HE LIKES THAT KIND OF A LETTER I COULD EVEN WRITE A BETTER ONE!

To: Orvie Snrkl
From: Gnrl Halftrck
Wd AGO 138704x I&E %.
LD40-53 Spei 745 (Par.B Wd Cir.
190, 1956) (Ar. 345-16)
Sr 600-370-1/4.
Initiate PDQ
BEAUTIFUL!
I'LL JUST LEAVE IT ON HIS DESK SO HE'LL BE SURE TO NOTICE IT!
I'LL BET HE'LL FLIP OVER IT
MORT WALKER
FALL OUT FOR ELBOW INSPECTION!
BREAKFAST WILL BE SERVED AT SUPPER
THE NEW UNIFORM WILL BE SNOWSHOES AND...
HE FINALLY FLIPPED
PHWEET
THE END

MY WATCH HAS STOPPED
IT MUST BE CLOSE TO FIVE O'CLOCK
WHEN IT'S THIS QUIET YOU KNOW EVERYBODY IS LISTENING FOR THE CHOW BELL

TIC
TOCK

HIC

BURP

SQUEAK!!

PUFF
MORT WALKER

HEY, SARGE! DID YOU HEAR ROCKY GOT A NEW AMPLIFIER?
THE END
4-14

BOY! AM I HUNGRY! BUT I DON'T DARE GO OFF MY DIET!
THE GENERAL IS WATCHING ME LIKE A HAWK
..OR A VULTURE

HOW'S YOUR DIET COMING, SARGE?
PRETTY GOOD, SIR

I HAVEN'T HAD A --
BONK

MESS
HALL

MORT
WALKER

IF YOU FINISH THAT PIE AND THEN GASP "WHERE AM I?" THE ANSWER IS, "YOU'RE IN TROUBLE!"
© King Features Syndicate, Inc., 1968. World rights reserved.
4-21

THE END

SHOW US HOW SARGE WOULD DO IT, SIR
OKAY
AWRIGHT, YOU BUMS! OL' SARGE SEZ TEN-HUT!!
YOU SHOULD BE ON TV WITH YOUR IMITATIONS, SIR
DO YOU REALLY THINK SO?
YEAH...IN THE REPAIR DEPARTMENT

AS JACKIE GLEASON SAYS, "AWAY WE GO!"
HERE'S HOW JOHN WAYNE GETS OUT OF A JEEP
WINSTON CHURCHILL HAD A WAY OF REVIEWING TROOPS THAT LENT A FIERCE PRIDE TO THE OCCASION.

BUT IT WAS HUMPHREY BOGART WHO COULD FACE ANY SITUATION WITHOUT LOSING HIS COOL
LIEUTENANT, THE GENERAL WANTS TO SEE YOU ABOUT YOUR GOOFING UP THE WAR GAMES YESTERDAY
MORT WALKER
SAY! THAT'S A GREAT IMITATION OF LT. FUZZ, SIR!
THE END

HERE'S YOUR COFFEE
CAREFUL! DON'T SPILL IT!
I WONDER WHO IS GOING TO GET IT TODAY. HE **ALWAYS** SPILLS COFFEE ON SOMEONE

OH, NO! HOT COFFEE ALL OVER MY PANTS.!!
BEETLE!
I DIDN'T DO IT!!
I KNOW
TAKE THESE PANTS TO MY ROOM AND BRING ME A CLEAN PAIR!
AND MAKE IT SNAPPY!!
WHAT'S ALL THE SHOUTING IN THERE?

DON'T YOU STAND UP WHEN A GENERAL ADDRESSES YOU?
ER-- DON'T YOU HAVE TO BE IN THE SAME ROOM, SIR?
5-5
I'LL COME INSIDE, THEN!
OH, FOR PETE'S SAKE!!
© King Features Syndicate, Inc., 1968. World rights reserved.
MORT WALKER
AND TO THINK THIS HAPPENED JUST BECAUSE I DIDN'T WANT TO BE SEEN IN MY SHORTS
WHERE ARE YOU?! BY GEORGE, IF I CATCH YOU I'LL WHIP THE PANTS OFF YOU!
THE END

WE'RE NOT HAVING EGGS FOR BREAKFAST, BEETLE
SARGE IS
HE NEEDED A COUPLE OF EGGS TO GET THE ENERGY TO TACKLE THOSE PANCAKES
AH! I FEEL INSPIRED!
A FULL TANK ALWAYS SEEMS TO MAKE A MOTOR RUN BETTER
MESS HALL

WHEN YOU PUT THAT SYRUP ON THE TOP SHELF, DID YOU SCREW THE LID ON TIGHT?
SURE! HERE, I'LL SHOW YOU!
GREAT! YOU BETTER TAKE A SHOWER QUICK BEFORE THAT STUFF HARDENS
OOPS!
I CAN HARDLY SEE WITH THAT SYRUP IN MY EYES

I BELIEVE THESE ARE SOME OF THE FINEST NOTICES I'VE EVER WRITTEN FOR THE BULLETIN BOARD
© King Features Syndicate, Inc., 1968. World rights reserved

WUNP

HOW DID YOU GET STUCK WITH THIS JOB, BEETLE?
BULLETIN BOARD
WELL, IT ALL STARTED WHEN I RAISED MY LEFT HAND AT THE INDUCTION CENTER
THE END
5-12

WHOOSH
WHOOSH
WHAT WAS THAT?

PX
PX

PX

Mort
WALKER

EITHER BEETLE IS GOOFING OFF AGAIN OR I'M IN THE EYE OF A HURRICANE
PX
The End
5-26

OH-OH! THERE'S LT. FUZZ'S SWAGGER STICK LYING ON THE GROUND
I MUST BE VERY CAREFUL NOT TO STEP ON IT
OOPS
CRACK
I DIDN'T MEAN TO!
I DIDN'T MEAN TO!
I DIDN'T MEAN TO!

BOY! IS LT. FUZZ MAD AT YOU FOR STEPPING ON HIS SWAGGER STICK
I DIDN'T MEAN TO BREAK IT
SO WHAT? HE SAID HE WAS GOING TO BEAT YOU TO A PULP ANYWAY!
THAT'S NOT FAIR! IF I HIT HIM BACK HE CAN COURT-MARTIAL ME
BETTER THINK OF SOMETHING! HERE HE COMES!
DEFEND YOURSELF, SARGE!
BIFF!
SOK!
OW!
UH!
TAP! TAP! TAP!
THUD!!

HIT!
CHUNK
POK!
POK!
POW!
HIT!
OOF!
GROAN
© King Features Syndicate, Inc., 1968. World rights reserved.
MORT WALKER
YOU'LL PAY FOR THIS, SNORKEL!
BUT YOU CAN'T COURT-MARTIAL HIM! HE NEVER HIT YOU
I KNOW! BUT HE TENSED UP! THAT'S WHAT HURT ME, HITTING ALL THOSE TENSED-UP MUSCLES.
the end
5-19

HYPNOTISM MADE EASY
WHY DO YOU WASTE TIME ON THAT JUNK?
WHAT WOULD YOU SAY IF IT HELPED US GET A MONTH'S LEAVE FROM SARGE?
HYPNOTISM MADE EASY
I'D SAY GO WAKE HIM UP AND TRY THAT JUNK RIGHT NOW!

HEY! LET'S SEE IF WE CAN HYPNOTIZE SARGE WHILE HE'S ASLEEP
YEAH
HYPNOTISM MADE EASY
ZZZ
YOU ARE UNDER MY POWER... YOU ARE UNDER MY POWER... YOU ARE UNDER MY POWER...
I AM UNDER YOUR POWER
I AM UNDER YOUR POWER
ZZZ
WHAT IS YOUR SECRET DESIRE? WHAT WOULD YOU REALLY LIKE TO BE ?
LOOK. HE'S ON ALL FOURS. HE THINKS HE'S A LION
BRRRRR
GRRRRR

BETTER BRING HIM OUT OF IT! HERE COMES THE GENERAL
WAKE UP, SARGE!
HUH?
© King Features Syndicate, Inc., 1968. World rights reserved.
BRRRRRRRR..
THEY TELL ME YOU WERE RUNNING UP AND DOWN THE AIR-STRIP CALLING FOR CLEARANCE
DRAT IT! I'M AN AIRPLANE! HAVE YOU ALL GONE CRAZY?
MP
MP
MORT WALKER
THE END

I WONDER WHAT BEETLE AND KILLER ARE DOING RIGHT NOW?
OW
WHERE ARE THOSE GUYS? IT'S TIME FOR LIGHTS OUT
THEY SHOULDN'T BE OUT WITH GIRLS AFTER DARK

LOOK! 3 A.M. AND HE'S STILL WAITING UP FOR US
Z
HE SURE WORRIES ABOUT US
HEY! LET'S GO AROUND AND SNEAK IN THE OTHER DOOR
GREAT! HE'LL BE UP ALL NIGHT! HEE HEE

WE MADE IT!
YEAH, WE UNDRESSED, BRUSHED OUR TEETH, PUT ON PAJAMAS, AND HE'S STILL WAITING

IT'S KIND OF A DIRTY TRICK, THOUGH, KEEPING HIM UP ALL NIGHT AFTER HE WAS SO CONCERNED ABOUT US
YEAH. LET'S GO TELL HIM WE'VE BEEN HERE AN HOUR
ARE YOU KIDDING? HE'D **KILL** US
WHAT CAN WE DO?
THIS IS STUPID! WE'LL EVEN HAVE TO BRUSH OUR TEETH AGAIN
BETTER THAN NOT **HAVING** TEETH
SO! HOME AT LAST!
STOMP
STOMP
CLANG!
THE END

WHAT A BEAUTIFUL DAY!
IT'S WINDY, CLOUDY AND COLD.. A **GREAT** DAY!
NO REFLECTIONS ON THE TABLE-- AND COOL ENOUGH FOR A GOOD HOT GAME
I FEEL LIKE I CAN HOLD MY SPOT ALL DAY AGAINST ALL COMERS

HEY, KILLER! WHADDYA SAY TO A GAME?
SORRY, SARGE! IN A RUSH! BIG DATE!
PONG
PONG
HEY, BEETLE!
BEE-TLE...
DOING ANYTHING, CAPTAIN SCABBARD?
PONG
PONG
SHH

OKAY, LT. FUZZ, I GUESS IT'S YOU
PHOOo! GET OUT OF HERE! YOU'VE BEEN EATING GARLIC AGAIN
PONG
PONG
PONG
PONG
PONG
PONG
MORT WALKER
© King Features Syndicate, Inc., 1968. World rights reserved.
I DON'T SUPPOSE YOU KNOW HOW TO KEEP SCORE
THE END
6-16

I'D LIKE TO CLARIFY THAT POINT, GENERAL HALFTRACK
US
I THINK GENERAL HALFTRACK APPRECIATES THE WAY I BRING UP QUESTIONS AT HIS MEETINGS
THE WAY TO GET AHEAD IN THE ARMY IS TO SHOW YOU'RE INTERESTED
AND I'M INTERESTED--
---IN GETTING AHEAD

I'LL PEPPER THE GENERAL WITH QUESTIONS AT HIS MEETING TODAY AND SHOW HIM I'M ON THE BALL!
HDQ
HMM. THEY MUST BE IN THE AUDITORIUM
MAYBE THEY DECIDED TO MEET IN THE GENERAL'S OFFICE

WHERE CAN THEY BE?

THE ONLY THING I CAN FIGURE IS THAT THIS MUST BE A TOP SECRET MEETING
MORT WALKER

TOP- TOP SECRET
LAUNDRY ROOM
THE END

YES, SIR.
RIGHT AWAY, SIR
THE GENERAL'S SECRETARY IS SICK. WHO CAN WE SEND TO HELP HIM?
PLATO WOULD BE GOOD
ON THE OTHER HAND, IT WOULD HELP ME IF I SENT ZERO

SARGE SAID YOU NEEDED ME BECAUSE YOU'RE SHORT-HANDED TODAY, SIR
THAT'S RIGHT
HOW LONG ARE YOUR HANDS USUALLY?
I'M IN NO MOOD FOR CORNY JOKES! HERE! FILE THESE!
I TOLD YOU NO CORNY JOKES! WHO EVER TOLD YOU YOU COULD DO OFFICE WORK?
THE DOCTOR.. MY FOOT IS SORE AND I COULDN'T GO ON THE HIKE TODAY

IT'S NICE OF YOU TO FEEL THIS WAY, SIR, BUT MY FOOT DOESN'T HURT THAT BAD. SEE?
GET OUT OF HERE!
AND TELL YOUR SERGEANT YOU'RE DRIVING ME TO THE PSYCHIATRIST'S COUCH!
MORT WALKER
YOU NEED THE JEEP?
YEAH. I'M SUPPOSED TO DRIVE THE GENERAL SOMEWHERE
© King Features Syndicate, Inc., 1968. World rights reserved.
6-30
THE END

THIS REPORT HAS TO BE FINISHED IMMEDIATELY, SARGE
YES, SIR
BETTER GET BUSY, BEETLE! THAT CEILING HAS TO BE PAINTED BEFORE THE INSPECTOR GENERAL ARRIVES!
YES, SIR
WATCH IT, BEETLE!
DON'T WORRY, SARGE! I'VE NEVER SPILLED PAINT ON YOU YET, HAVE I?

I KNOW HE'S GOING TO SPILL PAINT ON ME. HE ALWAYS DOES
THE ONLY TROUBLE IS-- WHEN?!

DURN BURN IT! I CAN'T CONCENTRATE ON ANYTHING ELSE
AND I GOTTA GET THIS REPORT DONE!
HERE! GIVE ME THAT CAN!
MORT WALKER
CLICK
CLICK
CLICK
CLICK
CLICK
CLICK
CLICK
7-7
THE END

AHEM..WE'RE ALL READY, SIR
READY FOR WHAT?
DON'T YOU THINK YOU SHOULD CALL THE MEETING TO ORDER, SIR?
WHAT MEETING ?
OH!...YES...UH... THE MEETING IS CALLED TO ORDER.

YOU'RE PROBABLY ALL WONDERING WHY I CALLED THIS MEETING... WELL... UH... HMM...DARN IT! I CAN'T SEEM TO REMEMBER
CAN ANYONE THINK WHY I MIGHT HAVE CALLED THIS MEETING?
HMM. WELL... UH... COFF! DISMISSED! I'LL, UH, RECALL YOU, UH, WHEN AND IF CONDITIONS WARRANT
© King Features Syndicate, Inc., 1968. World rights reserved.

HOW EMBARRASSING
I CAN'T REMEMBER THAT HAPPENING BEFORE
MAYBE I'D BETTER DISCUSS THIS WITH THE DOCTOR
WELL, GENERAL?
THE REASON I WANTED TO SEE YOU IS... UH.. --LE'S SEE.. HMMmm..
THE END

WRITE AUG. 3, 1968, ON THIS FOLDER AND PUT IT IN THE FILE
TODAY IS AUGUST FOURTH, SIR
1968 AUGUST
GROAN
GROAN
PX

MARTHA! GOOD! YOU WAITED UP FOR ME!
ALL THROUGH THE MEETING I KEPT THINKING, "I WISH I WERE HOME WITH MY MARTHA."
YOU LOOK LOVELY TONIGHT, MY DEAR
COME! GIVE ME A BIG KISS! I CAN'T RESIST YOUR CHARMS

MY LITTLE SOPHIA LOREN..
--HOW COULD ONE MAN BE SO LUCKY?
HEE HEE
I'LL BET I KNOW WHY YOU'RE BEING SO SWEET.. YOU REMEMBERED IT WAS OUR ANNIVERSARY
DIDN'T YOU?
NOT UNTIL THE PX WAS CLOSED
MORT WALKER
THE END

COME WITH ME, BEETLE
I NEED SOMEONE TO CARRY SOME STUFF FROM THE PX FOR ME
I'M BUSY. ASK SOMEONE ELSE
I DIDN'T **ASK** YOU TO COME WITH ME! I **TOLD** YOU TO COME WITH ME!

YOU TREAT ME LIKE A WORM OR SOMETHING!
THAT'S NOT TRUE, BEETLE
PX
YES, IT IS! YOU HAVE NO RESPECT FOR ME AS AN INDIVIDUAL! I'M JUST AN INSIGNIFICANT PIECE OF ARMY EQUIPMENT TO YOU!
KNOCK IT OFF
PX

THUNK
© King Features Syndicate, Inc., 1968. World rights reserved.

CRASH
TINKLE
THUD
BOP!
POW!

YOU OUGHTA GET THOSE BOTTLES OFF THE STEPS BEFORE SOMEONE GETS HURT
8-18 THE END

WE HAVE TO DO SOMETHING ABOUT THIS, SIR
I KNOW
LET'S GO TELL THE GENERAL
WHAT GOOD WILL THAT DO?
NO GOOD--BUT THEN IT WILL BE **HIS** PROBLEM, NOT **OURS**
GOOD THINKING

SIR, THE WAR GAMES ARE AT A DEAD HALT
A LITTLE OLD LADY IS HOEING HER GARDEN RIGHT IN THE BATTLE AREA
IMPOSSIBLE
SHE'S TOUGH, SIR
WE'LL SEE WHO'S TOUGH
I'VE **ALWAYS** HAD A GARDEN HERE, SONNY
MADAM, IF YOU DON'T LEAVE IMMEDIATELY I'LL --

YOU'LL WHAT?!
POW!
BUT, LADY! OW! LISTEN! OW!
GENERAL! WAIT! WHAT'LL WE DO?!
IT'S EVERY MAN FOR HIMSELF!
LISTEN TO THIS, SIR. "OLD LADY WINS WAR GAMES-- GENERAL AND TWO REGIMENTS ROUTED BY WOMAN WITH HOE."
PREPOSTEROUS! THEY OUGHT TO PRINT NONSENSE LIKE THAT ON THE COMIC PAGE!
THE END
MORT WALKER
9-1

THINK

THINK
THINK
THINK

THINK
HEY, SARGE! IF YOU TOOK THE "K" OFF THE END AND PUT IT IN FRONT, IT WOULD SPELL "KTHIN"
9-8

MORT WALKER
THE END

A TISKIT, A TASKET, A GREEN AND YELLOW BASKET..
TONIC
EIN, ZWEI, DREI, VIER, WHO'S GOING TO BUY THE BEER
TONIC

OH, GIVE ME A HOME WHERE THE BUFFALO ROAM
TOODLE UMA UMA TOODLE UMA UMA ANY UMBER-ELLAS TO FIX TODAY?
'WAY DOWN UPON THE S-WANEE RIVER..
FAR, FAR AWAY
TONIC
TONIC
TONIC

PACK UP YOUR TROUBLES IN YOUR OLD KIT BAG AND SMILE, SMILE, SMILE
TONIC
ROCK OF AGES, CLEFT FOR ME, LET ME HIDE MYSELF IN THEE
TONIC

IT'S A GRA
OLD FLAG, IT'S A HIGH FLYING FLAG
GOLLY! SARGE CAN WASTE MORE TIME IN THAT SHOWER!
© King Features Syndicate, Inc., 1968. World rights reserved.
10-13
THE END

THE LIEUTENANT SAID YOU HAD A JOB FOR US
YES, TAKE THIS CARD OVER TO THE SIGN SHOP
BOY, THAT'S THE ARMY FOR YOU
YEAH
THEY SEND TWO GUYS TO CARRY ONE PIECE OF PAPER

WANT TO SEE THE MILITARY MIND PERFORM?
MUST I?
SIR, THE GENERAL SAID THIS PIECE OF PAPER WAS WHITE, BUT---
HOLD IT, SOLDIER! IT'S NOT UP TO YOU TO QUESTION THE GENERAL!
IF HE SAID IT WAS WHITE HE PROBABLY HAD A VERY GOOD REASON!
AFTER ALL, WE OF THE RANK AND FILE CAN'T BE PRIVY TO THE SAME INFORMATION HE IS

IT MAY BE SOME SECRET WEAPON OR A DEVICE TO CONFUSE THE ENEMY
THE SECURITY OF OUR NATION COULD DEPEND ON THIS PIECE OF PAPER--PERHAPS THE WHOLE WORLD!
IF THE GENERAL SAYS THIS IS WHITE, DO YOU KNOW WHAT I SAY?
THIS PIECE OF PAPER IS WHITE!
© King Features Syndicate, Inc., 1968. World rights reserved.
10-20
THE END

YOUR GIRL IS HERE TO PICK YOU UP, KILLER
LUCKY GIRL
SIGH! I WISH I HAD A GIRL LIKE KILLER'S
WHY? IS SHE NICE?
I'LL SAY! 350 HORSEPOWER AND TWIN CARBURETORS!

BIRTH OF A NOTION
LET'S GO TO A MOVIE
AW, I'VE SEEN ALL THE LATEST PICTURES AT THE CAMP THEATER
HOW ABOUT A WALK IN THE PARK?
(GROAN) I WENT ON A 20-MILE HIKE YESTERDAY
SHALL WE GO BACK TO THE HOUSE AND PLAY CHECKERS?
THAT'S WHAT BEETLE AND I DO EVERY NIGHT

ISN'T THERE **ANYTHING** YOU DON'T DO AT THAT CAMP?!
HARDLY!

MAYBE I'D BETTER STOP HERE A MINUTE
© King Features Syndicate, Inc., 1968 World rights reserved

I'M SURE IF WE PUT OUR HEADS TOGETHER WE'LL THINK OF SOMETHING!
THE END

DING NAB IT! I DON'T SEE SGT. SNORKEL OR CAPT. SCABBARD ANYWHERE
THE ONLY OFFICER AROUND IS THAT JELLY-HEAD, LT. FUZZ
WELL, SOMEONE HAS TO CALL THE TROOPS TO ATTENTION
IT WOULDN'T BE DIGNIFIED FOR ME TO DO IT

LIEUTENANT, ORDER THE BATTALION TO ASSEMBLE
ME, SIR?
OH, BOY! YES, SIR!
© King Features Syndicate, Inc., 1968. World rights reserved.
ATTALION BASSEMBLE!!
HA! HA!
HEE HEE
STOP LAUGHING!
LIEUTENANT! YOU'RE SPLASHING MUD ON ME!

I'M SORRY, SIR! HERE! I'LL WASH IT OFF!
LIEUTENANT!... ATTENTION!!!

WHAK!
INCREDIBLE! IS HE ALWAYS THIS FLUSTERED IN FRONT OF THE TROOPS?
11-3

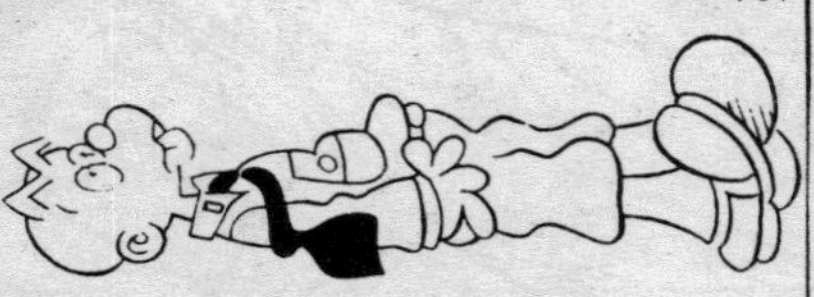
ONLY AT FIRST, SIR. THEN HE BECOMES VERY CALM.. JUST AS YOU SEE HIM NOW
MORT WALKER

THE END

THERE ARE SOME GOOD IDEAS IN THIS BOOK
EXERCISE the YOGA WAY
US
BY JINGO! I'M GOING TO WRITE OUT A PROGRAM OF EXERCISES FOR MYSELF...
EXERCISE the YOGA
IF I CAN GET SOMEONE TO SHARPEN MY PENCIL
US

DRAT IT! WHERE DID THAT PENCIL ROLL TO?
WHAT'S HE DOING NOW?
HE'S BEEN READING A YOGA BOOK. IT'S PROBABLY A REJUVENATING EXERCISE
HA HA! I'D LIKE TO SEE AN EXERCISE THAT WOULD REJUVENATE **HIM!**
BUNK

YOW

WHOEEEEEEE

HEE HEE HEE
HEE HA HEE
HEE
HEE
HEE
HEE

WHEW! THAT WAS LIKE AN ELECTRIC SHOCK!
US

HEY! YOU ALL SHOULD HAVE SEEN ME WHEN I HIT MY FUNNY BONE...
MORT WALKER
THE END

ANYONE WHO WANTS TO GO TO TOWN CAN GO
AREN'T YOU GOING WITH US, BEETLE?
NO. I'M GONNA STAY IN THE BARRACKS AND RELAX.
OH-OH! I FORGOT I NEEDED SOMEONE TO CLEAN THE CAPTAIN'S OFFICE
I WONDER IF ANYONE IS IN THE BARRACKS?

I NEED ONE VOLUNTEER!
I THOUGHT I HEARD SOMEONE IN HERE
WHAT WAS THAT?

NOPE
I GUESS I WAS WRONG. THERE'S NO ONE IN HERE
© King Features Syndicate, Inc., 1968. World rights reserved
MORT WALKER
ON THE OTHER HAND, BEDS AND WALLS DON'T BREATHE HEAVILY, DO THEY?
THE END
10-6

GENERAL HALFTRACK
(SIGH)
GENERAL HALFTRACK
ANYTHING WRONG, SIR?
NO! THERE'S NOTHING AT ALL WRONG!
EVERYTHING IS DANDY!
JUST DANDY!

IS THE PENTAGON DEAD?!
HALFTRACK HASN'T HEARD FROM it For FIVE YEArS *

SNORKEL! HAVE THAT WASHED OFF IMMEDIATELY!

IF THE PENTAGON EVER HEARD ABOUT THAT THEY'D BE **FURIOUS**!
US

THEY'D SEND INVESTIGATORS! THEY'D WRITE BLISTERING LETTERS! THEY'D TELEGRAPH--

THEY'D..

IS THE PENTAGON DEAD?
2-18
THE END

Z
GRINDDDDDDDDDD
CHOMP
ZZ
Z
Z
Z Z

Z
Z
Z
Z
Z
GRINNODD
CHOMP
CHOMP
SNIFF
ZN
Z
ZZZ

BOY! SARGE MAKES SO MUCH NOISE I CAN'T SLEEP!

THIS IS BETTER OVER HERE
I CAN'T HEAR HIM AT ALL

URK! URK!
OOOOOOOOOOOOO
SNAP!
GRONK!
FLUTTER
EEEEEEEEEEEEEE
7-28
MORT WALKER

© King Features Syndicate, Inc., 1968. World rights reserved.
Z
Z
GRIND
CHOMP SNIFF
Z
THE END

WHO DID THIS?!
NOT ME
SNORKEL

BEETLE DID IT!!
BEETLE DID IT!!
SNORKEL

LOOK OUT, BEETLE!

HIT HIM! HIT HIM, BEETLE!!

KICK HIM!
KICK HIM!

BITE!! BITE!!

SCRATCH HIM, BEETLE!

WUPS! OUT OF PAINT
I'LL LEAVE THE CAN THERE SO I'LL KNOW WHERE I STOPPED
DARN BEETLE! FIRST HE MISSES PUTTING A SECOND COAT ON SOME OF THE WINDOWS AND **NOW** HE LEAVES AN EMPTY CAN OUT HERE!

BOY! HE MAKES ME MAD!
WAIT'LL I FIND HIM!
POW
HEY! THE CAN'S GONE! I MARKED THE WINDOW I WAS SUPPOSED TO PAINT WITH THAT EMPTY CAN
NOW I'LL HAVE TO FEEL AROUND ALL THE WINDOWS TO---
?
HEY! MAYBE I'M ON THE WRONG SIDE OF THE BARRACKS

IT'S BACK AGAIN!! I'M GOING TO KICK THAT CAN FROM HERE TO CHINA!
SARGE WANTS TO SEE YOU
WHAT'S HE KICKING ABOUT NOW?
MORT WALKER
9-9
©King Features Syndicate, Inc., 1973. World rights reserved.

THE END

THERE'S NOTHING TO DO AROUND HERE
WHAT DID YOU SAY, BEETLE?
HUH? OH...ER... NOTHING, SARGE. I WAS JUST CLEARING MY THROAT
BEETLE, IF YOU'RE LOOKING FOR SOMETHING TO DO, TAKE THIS BULLETIN BOARD TO THE SHOP AND FIX IT
DO I LOOK LIKE I'M LOOKING FOR SOMETHING TO DO?

OH-OH! I'D BETTER HURRY AND GET THIS BOARD BACK UP
THAT WAS FAST
AM I TOO LATE?
TOO LATE FOR WHAT ?
OH, YOU KNOW HOW PLATO ACTS WHEN HE SEES AN EMPTY WALL
9-2
MORT WALKER

TOO LATE
Pretend this is your last day
crusts to the birds...Polish
slowly and see things..Buy
or matchbooks, or rocks
the dictionary...Play
re-read it -- Study
your shoes--Make
Practice smiling in a
the whole day." There's

on earth...go down to the water and feed bread
a table.. walk to town for a change...walk
a mouse. Let it go... Start a button collection,
...Begin a diary... Learn 10 new words from
an old record...Find your favorite poem and
a leaf in the light... Shine all
some popcorn...wash a car...
mirror...Don't say once during
nothing to do around here!"

THE END

SARGE, I'VE MADE A LIST OF ALL MY COMPLAINTS
GIVE ME THAT!
NOW TAKE YOUR COMPLAINTS AND PUT THEM WHERE YOU SHOULD HAVE PUT THEM IN THE FIRST PLACE
© King Features Syndicate, Inc., 1968. World rights reserved.

MORT WALKER
9-22
GENERAL HALFTRACK
THE END

TRY TO KEEP THE NOISE DOWN, YOU GUYS

DO EITHER OF YOU HAVE AN ASPIRIN?
THERE'S A BOTTLE ON MY SHELF

OTTO HAS A HANGOVER

"FIRST, IT WAS MAKING THAT LITTLE BED FOR HIM---"

"THEN HE HAD A LITTLE UNIFORM MADE AND TAUGHT HIM TO SIT AT HIS OWN LITTLE DESK---"

"NOW OTTO WALKS ON HIS HIND LEGS AND GOES **EVERYWHERE** WITH SARGE---"